Calibri

And

Bold

By Hannah Willey

DEDICATION:

To anyone who's ever felt like
they don't belong, just wait;
your story is only beginning to
unfold.

Don't give up before you've
seen what you'll become.

~ Calibri And Bold ~

Gentle light,
Softly dim,
Reading the pages,
Worn as skin.

Shining black soldiers,
Calibri and Bold,
Telling a story,

One so very old.

~ Heart Stains ~

Love is not an abscess,
Waiting to be drained.

Love is just a canvas,
Waiting to be stained.

~ Judging A Book By
Its' Cover ~

The covers that we read,
Are just people covering up.

So please,

Before you throw away the book,

Just look,

And let them off the hook.

~ Aristotle's Fossil ~

Listen to me,
If your mind is not playing its
part,
Remember this.

If Aristotle believed that a
dropped rock
Fell to the Earth because it
belonged there,

Then surely you can believe the
same of yourself.

You are wanted, and beautiful
too, and I promise you it's true.

~ Lemon Drop Love ~

What they don't tell you is that a
love that tastes like lemon drops,

Is bitter,

Not sweet.

~ Sweet Lies ~

You said you'd never lie.

'I love you' you'd say.

But that was the first lie

You told me today

~ Waiting Game ~

Sometimes it feels like I'm just
waiting for time to pass,
Like I'm sitting on the outside
peering in through the glass,
But other times you get these
moments,
Like when you're swimming in
the Ocean,
Or listening to a class,
And suddenly you're back on the
path,
And no longer do you grow
weary,
Waiting for your story to start.

~ Breathe ~

I keep myself busy,

I keep breathing,

I do.

But at the end of the day,
I feel nothing without you.

~ Heartbeat Receipt ~

Your heart will beat until the day
you die,

So it's okay to not to worry,

And to just spend time with the
sky.

~ Game ~

Love is not a game,

People can't be played.

Life is not for fame,

It's for stories to be made.

~ Soul ~

You are just a soul,
And changing the way you look
in the mirror will not make you
feel any more whole.
So every insta body that you
scroll,
Should never be allowed to take
a toll.

~ Fairytale ~

Pretty Aurora
On a spindle she's pricked
Awoken one day
By the kiss of her prince

But gentle Aurora
Why must this be so
Wasn't this story written
Years and Years ago?

~ Love Is The Stuff Of
Dreams ~

He promised he'd love me,
He promised he'd stay.

Then I rolled out of bed,

And the dream tumbled away.

~ Shout Me ~

Shoot me down and I will bleed,
But shout me down and I will
lead.

~ Broken Dreams ~

It's the dreams that can never fit
together,
The ones that push and shove
until they break,

That are the often ones that
needed something new
altogether,

And the breaking of them is what
fits them back into place.

~ Reaching Away ~

Plants reach towards the sun,

Yes,

But that doesn't mean they hide
from the moon.

Reach for the things that bring
you joy,

But in trying so hard to avoid the
darkness,

Do not risk missing the light.

~ Misogyny ~

Your beauty is not in the way you
cross your legs when you sit down,

It is not in the way you say "excuse
me" after every noise, so not to
cause a frown,

It is not in the way you smother
your jokes, or hide your blokes,

Because women should not act like
such a "clown",

You are not just beautiful, but
powerful, and one day we will
watch this misogyny drown.

~ Don't Worry About
Others ~

Don't worry about others,

No one has your hair,

Your eyes,

Your face,

So of course we are all going at
our own special pace.

~ No Grow ~

Stop waiting for people to agree
with you,

Don't let someone else be the
reason you never grew.

~ Burning The Candle At Both Ends ~

"You're burning the candle at both ends",

Yes but didn't anyone ever tell you,

Candles are made to be burned.

~ Kinder Hearts ~

They tell us that our teeth should
be whiter,
Our abs should be tighter.

I just think that our hearts could
be kinder.

Especially to our minds.

~ Learn To Love Yourself ~

No matter where you travel to,
Who you cling to,
You will always be the person
you were when you cried that
first cry, until you breathe your
last breath.

So learn to love that dimpled
smile,

Because you will be with it for
quite a while.

~ God Of The Sky ~

I bet even Zeus,
The God Of The Sky,
Wanted to float up and away
sometimes.

~ Goddess Of Love ~

I bet even Aphrodite,
The Goddess Of Love,
Had her heart broken a few
times.

~ Housing Market ~

We spend our nights sat in
brickwork boxes,

And our lives paying off the
mortgages for them.

~ Loophole ~

Everything you are is made to
divide us,
From the colour of your hair,
To how much money you have to
spend on the bus,

But it does not have to be so,

The rich can be humble of heart,
The poor can be rich in soul,

We will find a loophole.

~ Deathbed ~

You will never lie on your
deathbed,

Wishing you had worked more
hours and made more money,

You will wish you had seen how
rich you already were,

You will wish it hadn't taken you
so long to realise that your
wealth is not measured in paper.

~ Surely ~

Your skirt is too short,
Your hair is too curly,

I think that women deserve more
than that,

Surely.

~ Journey In The Sand ~

Footsteps on a path often do not
leave a mark,
But with footsteps in the sand
you leave your journey in the
land,

Be like sand,

Carry your story in the lines of
your hand.

~ Why Are You Crying? ~

Why are you crying? Are you
sad?
The little boy asked the old man,
And the old man looked to the
sunset dancing over the sky and
he said,
"The sky is so beautiful,
Yes,
I am sad,
Because I held these tears in my
entire life,
I pushed them down until they
poured out into anger,
Seeping into my love,
Into my life,
A black cloud,

When all I needed to do,
Was to look to the sunset,
And let my tears feel the beauty
on their backs,
Let them melt into my skin like
butter,
Let them extinguish so they
could cause no more pain,
But now the pain has already
burnt,
The welts are left,
And my tears can be pushed
down no longer"

~ Nothing But A Test ~

We stress,
So often,
Over little things like buying the
right dress,
Or trying to look our very best,
When really,
Life is nothing but a test,

And the way that you look will
never make you score any less.

~ Becoming The Light ~

In searching through the
darkness,

I found you.

In becoming the light,

I outgrew you.

~ Heart To Mind,
Body To Soul ~

There is a kindness in my heart,

And love within my soul,

Yet when I am without you,

Still,

I am not whole.

~ Insignificant Lifetimes,
Beautiful Skylines ~

Sometimes it takes staring to the
distance at a blackened star,

For us to realise how small we
are.

~ Foolproof Dreamer ~

The fool who dares to dream,

Is not a fool at all.

~ Cover To Cover ~

'Powerful' 'Exquisite'

'A joy to read'

And all the onyx soldiers did,

Was stand still and bleed

~ Vast Moon ~

When you look at the moon and
see how big and beautiful it is,
And you look on its vastness
with joy,
So why is it when you look in the
mirror,
You see a larger size as
something to destroy.

~ Lips ~

The shape of her hips,
The kiss of her lips,
She was full of beauty they
would say,
But the quip of her tongue,
The most powerful one,

Was what scared all the good
ones away.

~ Eyes Of The Soul ~

Look into the eyes of the people
you love,
Stare until you see the makings
of their soul,
And you'll realise that,
Everyday,
There is something in them that
makes you whole.

~ Flower In The Wind ~

A flower blowing in the wind
Knows that the soil will always
keep it pinned,
So it lets itself grow,
It has space to flow,
It frees it's colours to dance in
the wind.

So be like a flower,
Remember your power,

Feel your roots even when you
grow leaves.

~ Birthday ~

I just find it so cool how we take
one day out of our year,
Every year,
To celebrate the day we were
born with all the people we hold
dear.

~ A Wave Of Freedom ~

And as I watched the waves
crash through the sea,

I looked around and realised that
there was no one else I'd rather
be,

And that is what truly set me
free.

~ Rainbow ~

Yes the rain will be back,

Tomorrow,

But you gotta hang on for the
rainbow.

~ Stepping Stones ~

Keep walking towards the things
that make you happy,
The things that make your soul
scream with joy,
And one day,

You will reach the place you've
been trying so hard to find.

~ Met With A Rhyme ~

We are all just floating,
After age,
After time.

And every emotion,
Can be met with a rhyme.

~ A Question Of Life ~

We spend our days asking about everyone else's lives,

And our nights crying over our own.

~ Your Mind Is Not Your
Fault ~

Your mind is not your fault,
So it's okay when you just need
everything to halt,

Take the world as your vault.

Let your soul be full of sugar, not
salt.

~ The Jungle ~

In the jungle,
Birds cry to their mothers,
Snakes hiss at their wives,
And here we are crowning
ourselves Kings,
Controlling the Earth,
Yet doing the exact same things.

~ What Is Normal? ~

What is normal anyway?
I'd choose different over normal
any day,
We are not here to look
"perfect",
We are not sculpted out of clay,
We are just ourselves,

That's the way it should be,
anyway.

~ What A Mad World ~

Lights off,
Doors closed,
Sleepless nights,
Children unclothed.
But that's just the world we live
in,

I suppose.

~ Adulthood ~

A screaming child will get hugs
and kisses,
A screaming adult will get
hushes and whispers,
A laughing baby will giggle until
its lungs grow wings and fly,
A laughing adult will laugh until
they finally let the tears go and
they cry.

~ Drownings Of The Heart ~

My heart contains the teardrops
of the world,

I cannot let you in.

You would drown.

~ So Tired ~

I'm tired,

I am so tired

Of feeling like I need to be
desired,
Like I need to be hired,

When really,

In this life,

Nothing but love is required.

~ Mirror Me ~

I'm starting to see,
That the person I will always be,
Is the person who is standing in the
mirror right in front of me,
And she's been there since I was 3
and I cried when I fell and hurt my
knee,
She was there when I ached for my
mother until my face was red and
blotchy,
She will even be there when I'm
stressed out about bills at thirty,
Because there is a woman in the
mirror, and I know that no matter
what she looks like, that woman will
always have a heart as wide and deep
as the sea,
And that woman is the woman who I
always will be.

~ Anything Goes ~

Chicken nugget,
Bargain bucket,

You see,
Anything can be a poem if it has
the same suffix.

~ Your Home ~

Sometimes,

The person that you call your
home,

Doesn't want to be the place
where your love resides,

Sometimes,

They want only to be free to
roam.

~ At Night ~

At night you wonder,

And you wonder if you're doing
it,
Doing anything, right.

And I'm here to tell you that it's
alright.

You don't have to be fuelled with
that powerful might,
You don't have to want to fight
and fight and fight.

Sometimes your only purpose is
to dance and sing with the light.

~ A Child's Prayer ~

Poetry holds the answers to the questions that children are too frightened to ask.

~ Broken Heart ~

When you fall and hurt your
knee,
And feel the blood rolling across
your skin,
You find a plaster, rest and tend
to its needs,

So why when your heart is
broken do you continue to try to
run at full speed?

~ Dear Writer ~

Dear writer,

Never forget that you are as
powerful with a pen in your hand
as a solider with a gun or a
doctor in demand.

So any problem or sadness you
feel in your heart,

Can be written,

And that is always where the best
stories will start.

~ Life Cycle ~

A plant from a seed, a chicken
from an egg,
Once you've seen where you
come from
You'll feel no more dread.

~ Searching ~

The things you look for in others,

Love, Strength, Forgiveness,

Are so often just the things you
need to find in yourself.

~ We Are Being Played ~

The images that surround me,
That drown me every single day,
And for millions of others this
story is exactly the same.
It's a game.
We are being played.
The beauty we see on the
everyday,
The timeline I scroll,
Wasting away the days,
It's insane.
But it doesn't have to be this
way.

~ You Are ~

You are not the things you have
seen,
You are not the people you have
loved,
You are made of so much beauty
and power,

You are sent from above.

~ The Lives We Lead ~

We paint our pretty faces,
We spit our little lies,
We run to all our favourite
places,
We stuff our faces with pies,
We dream about being famous,
And then we huddle up and die.

Why?

~ Hate The Player Not
The Game ~

I hate that about you,
The way everything moves to
you,
Like you are a magnet,

Like we are just pawns in your
game,

But mostly I hate that I miss you,
I hate that I still want to kiss you,

Hate that I still so want to be
played.

~ A Vision ~

I have a vision,
For a world without division,
A world where love is given,
Where people do nothing but
listen.

Listen to their hearts,
Listen to their souls;
And no one tries to take
control.

~ Hidden Parts, Broken Hearts ~

I hid myself away,
Deep in the shadows of the
Earth,
Then I cried because nobody
could find me.

Little did I know,
I first had to find myself.

~ Between Your Ears ~

Be with someone who loves
what's between your ears,

And not just what's between
your legs.

~ Begin Again ~

Take me back to my roots,
Peel away my skin,
Plant me like a flower,
Let me find the courage to
begin.

~ Time To Stop Caring ~

It's time to stop caring what
other people think,
So dance in the street,
Dye your hair pink,

Keep on singing to your
heartbeat.

~ Hug Them ~

Hug them until they can't
breathe,

At least they'll know they were
loved until their last breath.

~ Doors ~

He spent a lifetime closing doors,

Then a fortnight wondering why
there were no doors left open.

~ Soul Searching ~

Why do you search so hard,
For the things that are already
there.

Your soul has not gone missing,

It's just soaring through the air.

~ Little Old Town ~

If you stand up they tell you to sit
down,
If you treat yourself like a
Queen,
They will try to take your crown,
But don't you frown,

Because you are more than what
you will find in this little old
town.

~ Plant Life ~

A broken plant pot must first be
fixed,
Before it can hold the weight of a
new plant.

Give yourself time to heal.

~ Memory ~

One day all this will just be a memory,

So breathe it all in,

Fill it with your energy.

~ Nothing's Forever ~

Nothing's forever,
So buy that sweater,
Send that letter,

And never forget that there is no
storm you cannot weather.

~ Checking ~

Check your emails,
Check the time,
We live in in a world where we
are constantly checking things,

I say check yourself out once in a
while.

Because you are beautiful.

~ Just Live ~

Be patient,
Treat your life as vacation:
Yes,
There are places to be and people
to see,

But the most important part is to
let go of all your frustrations.

And just live.

~ Lost And Found ~

Don't worry about finding
yourself,
You are already found,
A lost flip flop in the ocean is not
lost,
It is just further away.

You are not lost,

You are just taking a swim.

~ Heaven Sent ~

The books that you read,
And the pictures that you paint,
Will somehow,
One day,

Make you a saint.

~ See ~

You are not what you see in the
mirror,
You are made of what you
cannot see.

And under the skin you so wish
was clearer,

Are the thousands of vessels that
beat with that guarantee.

~ Eyes ~

They say that a persons' eyes are
the window to their soul.

Funny how yours were always
closed.

~ Betrayal ~

I laid all my cards,
I thought you had too.

But what I didn't realise,

Was that you'd used mine as
glue.

~ Stars ~

All stars die.
But right now.

Right now.

Their light is the most beautiful
thing you can see.

Everything in this life one day
leaves,

But I think that's just part of
what makes us free.

~ Opposites Attract ~

The glow of moon was in his
eyes,
But the fire of the sun was in her
heart.
Opposites attract she cries,
But the moon had already done
its' depart.

~ Grass Seems Greener ~

Yes, the grass always seems
greener,
In someone else's life,
But that doesn't mean it's clearer,

Sometimes trouble is hidden in
strife.

~ Free To Express ~

We should be free to express
without being oppressed,

Without that aching fear in your
chest,

Of your wounds being undressed.

~ Voice In Your Head ~

When the voice inside your head
gets too loud,

Don't you frown,

You were not put here to
drown.

~ Clean Hands, Clean Heart ~

Clean hands,
Clean heart,

Yet here I am, still waiting for
the adventure to start.

~ One Day ~

Hold on,
Even when it feels like you are
ripping into two,
It's okay to feel blue,
It's okay to need to chat and have
a brew,

But hold on,

Because one day,
It will all shift,

And you will feel anew.

~ Hidden Figures ~

I walk with the shadows,
So that I can see you reach the
light.

I sleep in the meadows,
So I can see your face in the stars
of the night.

~ Skylines And Lifelines ~

Lipstick is red,
Skylines are blue,
I want to see the world,

And I want you there too.

~ Learning ~

I'm learning how to dance to my
own beat,
Learning how to love what I eat,
Learning how to sing on the high
street,
I'm letting the things that would
break me, wake me.

Because I won't forsake me.

~ Broken Laughter ~

I searched for someone else,
I tried to paint your smile in the
echo of their laugh,
But it just fades,

Because without you,

Everything falls apart.

~ Library Of My Mind ~

A library full of books,
And you chose me.

Thank you for looking,
And stopping at me.

~ Do Not Seek, See ~

Look carefully,
And you will see,
The people who light up a room
are not the people who need it,
The people who seek it,
Who ache for it like an addict for
their next hit,
It is the people who do not care
for it,
The people who do not allow
their emotions to be controlled
by another's approval.

Do not seek and it will come.

~ Breathe In, Breathe Out, Shake It All About ~

Breathe in,
Breathe out,
That's what it's all about.
Nothing that has been,
Will be,
Or anything else that makes you doubt,
Can hurt you,
So let yourself go,
And shake it all about.

~ Heatstroke, Heart Broke ~

I'm falling asleep,
Wanting to weep.
I'm feeling the heat,
Because without you,

I am incomplete.

~ Golden Crown ~

Never again will I let my
thoughts hold me down,
Pushing and pushing until I feel
myself start to drown,
Yes,
I will let myself frown,
But then I will get up and fix my
golden crown.

~ See Me ~

One day you will see,
In the time you spent searching
for someone to love you,
In the tears you cried because
there was no one beside you,
You looked past me,

And while you were talking
about him,

I was waiting for you to see me.

~ Homeward Bound ~

Empty trains,
Winding lanes,
The fragments of a home that
will forever weave inside my
veins.
And there will be no bloodstains,
No campaigns,
Only beautiful heart strains,
That will move and dance when
the sky rains.

~ Cattle Battle ~

We are the cattle,
And they are the prods,
We try so hard to escape,
But see how slim the odds?

~ You Said ~

You always said I'd never be
enough,
You told me that the world would be
better if I just shut up,
And for so long I let your words
keep me trapped like handcuffs,
But the markings you left on my
wrists, on my soul,
They made it harder and harder to
find me a loophole.

And yet they made me tough.
So tough that now today,
I can stand here and say,
I don't care what you have to say,

I like myself better this way.

~ Why Do We Do This To
Ourselves ~

I loved you more than I loved
myself,
For you I locked myself away,
confined to a shelf,
Just like those little old
Christmas elves.

Stupid humans,
Why do we do this to ourselves.

~ It's The Little Things ~

I'm learning to pick up the
pieces,
I'm starting to see that life is not
always fresh green leaves and
soft white beaches,
Sometimes you find your joy in
things like doing the dishes,
Or stealing away kisses.

And that is always,

How we should measure our
riches.

~ Broken Body,
Fractured Mind ~

Please don't break my body,
It's only starting to heal.
It was my mind that broke it,
When all along,
My mind was thing that was
broken,
My only fault was thinking my
body was broken just for looking
different.
For having brighter hair, darker
teeth and every other claim.

When really no body, nobody is
every truly the same.

~ The Journey Within ~

What you are within,
Is more than you will ever be
without,
So when you feel like crying,
When you want to scream and
shout,
Let yourself be free of worry,
Feel your mind escape from
doubt,
Because,
Honestly,
We are all still just working it
out.

~ A Dove ~

You are connected and you are
so loved,

And one day, quite soon,

You'll fly up, like a dove.

Printed in Great Britain
by Amazon

65469526R00071